CARL REINER

Tell Me a

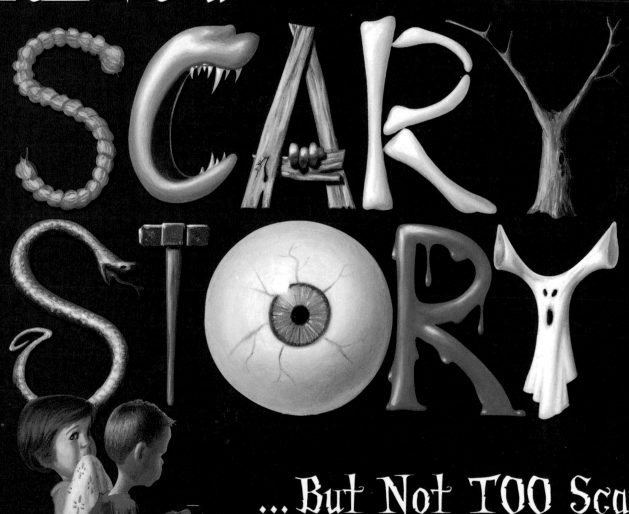

SCARY STORY

...But Not TOO Scary!

ILLUSTRATED BY **JAMES BENNETT**

LITTLE, BROWN AND COMPANY
New York   Boston

A Byron Preiss Book

To Nick
—C.R.
To my best inspirations, Steven and Brett
—J.B.

Little, Brown and Company

Hachette Book Group
237 Park Avenue, New York, NY 10017
Visit our website at www.lb-kids.com

First Paperback Edition: September 2007
First published in hardcover in September 2003 by Little, Brown and Company

Library of Congress Cataloging-in-Publication Data
Reiner, Carl.
Tell me a scary story—but not too scary! / by Carl Reiner; illustrated by James Bennett.—1st ed.
p. cm.
"A Byron Preiss book."
Summary: A little boy has an adventure in the scary basement of his mysterious new neighbor,
Mr. Neewollah.
ISBN 978-0-316-83329-5 (hc) / ISBN 978-0-316-00260-8 (pb)
[1. Monsters—Fiction. 2. Neighbors—Fiction.] I. Bennett, James, ill. II. Title.
PZ7.R27487 Te 2003
[E]—dc21   2002031282

HC: 10 9 8 7 6 5 4 3 2 1
PB: 10 9 8 7 6 5 4 3

SCP

Printed in China

Before we begin . . .

I hope you'll like this story, but if it gets too scary for you, just say, "Stop reading!" and I'll stop, because I love you very much.

I like people who smile, but I didn't like Mr. Neewollah's smile.
It was a crooked, mysterious smile.

This isn't too scary for
you, is it?
I didn't think so.
I'll go on.
I stood behind a tree
and watched him
carry a large box
into his house.
Something shiny fell
out and rolled across
the street. It stopped
at my feet. I picked it
up, shoved it in my
pocket, and ran
home. I couldn't wait
to see what it was.

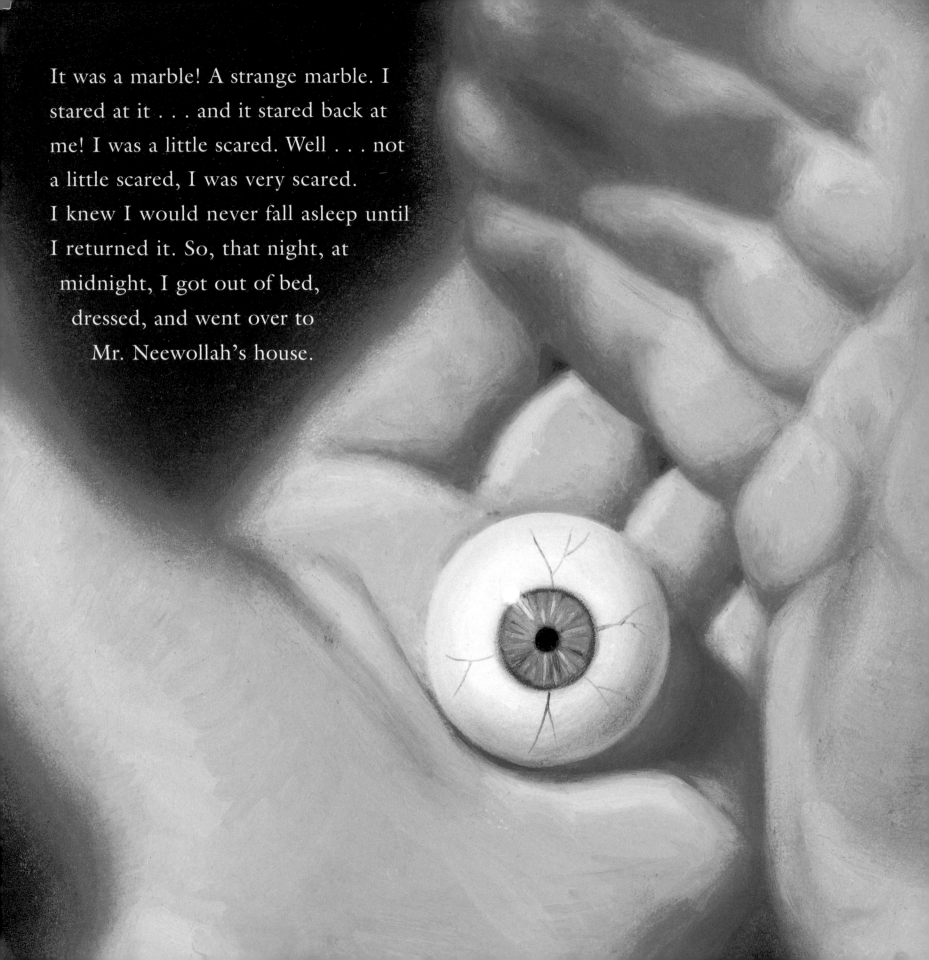

It was a marble! A strange marble. I
stared at it . . . and it stared back at
me! I was a little scared. Well . . . not
a little scared, I was very scared.
I knew I would never fall asleep until
I returned it. So, that night, at
midnight, I got out of bed,
dressed, and went over to
Mr. Neewollah's house.

The house was dark except for a small light coming from the basement. I knelt down and looked in. I saw something covered with a cloth. It looked like something really creepy so I shut my eyes!

Is it getting too scary for you?
Should I keep going? Okay, if you say so.

I leaned in closer, but before I knew it, the
window flew off its hinge and I fell inside!

Slowly I opened my eyes and there, on a chair, was that creepy thing covered with a cloth! I wanted to get out of there!

Before I could get out, there was a voice behind me.

"WHAT ARE YOU DOING HERE?"

I turned and saw the smiling

JOHN NEEWOLLAH.

"I . . . . I was looking in to see if
you were home," I stuttered.
"I'm your neighbor. We met earlier . . ."
"YES," he said, suspiciously,
"SO, WHY ARE YOU HERE
NOW?
DON'T YOU KNOW NEVER TO
GO INTO A STRANGER'S
HOUSE ALONE?"
"I know, my mom and dad told me that.
I came to return *this*," I said,
handing him the marble.

He looked at the staring marble—then he stared at me.

"It's . . . uh . . . a very interesting marble," I said.

"INDEED," he said, smiling his crooked smile.

"I HAVE MANY INTERESTING THINGS.
WOULD YOU LIKE TO SEE THEM?" he asked.

Is it getting too scary for you?
Should I keep going?
Okay, if you say so.

"BE VERY CAREFUL," Mr. Neewollah said, smiling that smile. "THE STAIRS ARE STEEP. I WOULDN'T WANT YOU TO TUMBLE DOWN." He gave me a look that sent shivers down my spine.

He took my arm . . . and I grabbed the
railing. The stairs creaked and the light
got dimmer and dimmer.

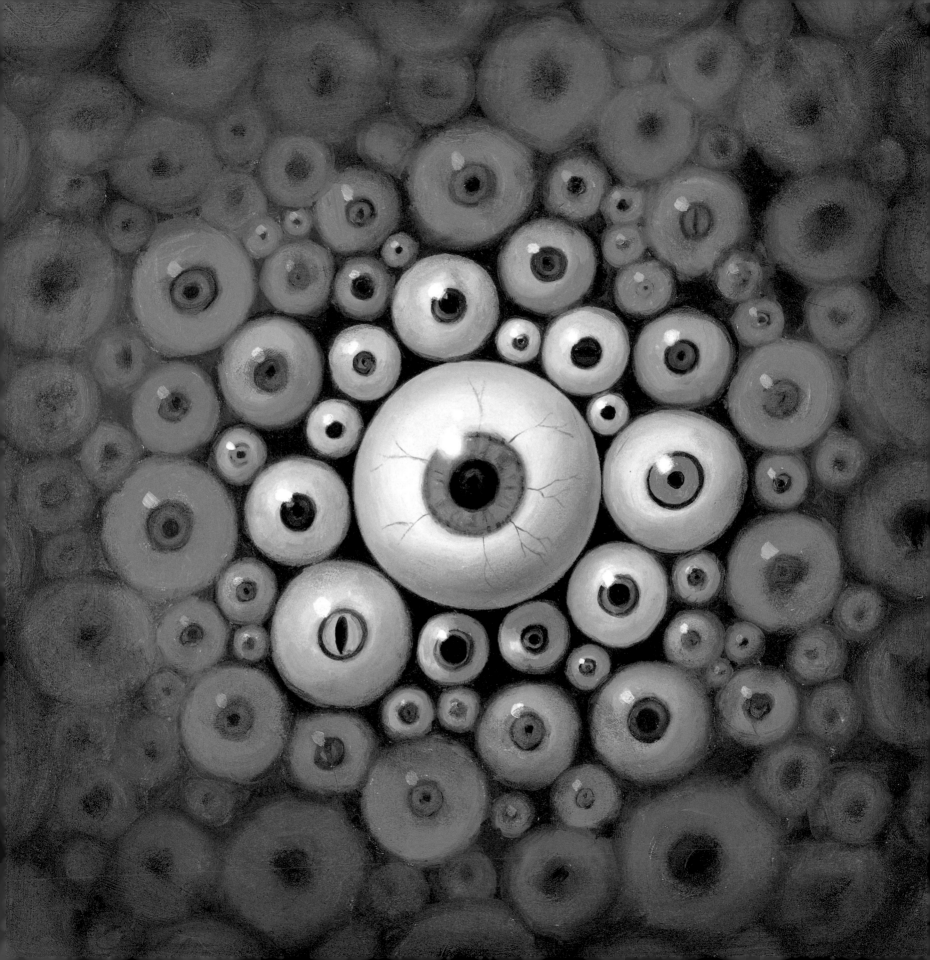

Mr. Neewollah led me to his work table. Then he turned on a light. There, on the work table, were **HUNDREDS** of staring marbles—all staring directly at me! I felt like I was being watched by hundreds of **COLD, DEAD EYES.**

"DO THEY LOOK FAMILIAR?"

he asked.

Before I could answer, he grabbed two of the marbles. Then he picked up something weird from under the black cloth and ran up the stairs.

"DON'T MOVE!" he shouted, "THERE'S SOMEONE I WANT YOU TO MEET!"

He laughed maniacally and slammed the door shut.

I WAS TRAPPED!

Suddenly, the light went out . . . I heard a door creak . . .
and then . . . strange, scary noises came out of the dark. . . .

Something with red beams of light shooting from its eyes was coming down the basement stairs. It came closer and closer . . . the hair on the back of my neck was sticking
straight out. I finally saw it—and it was alive!

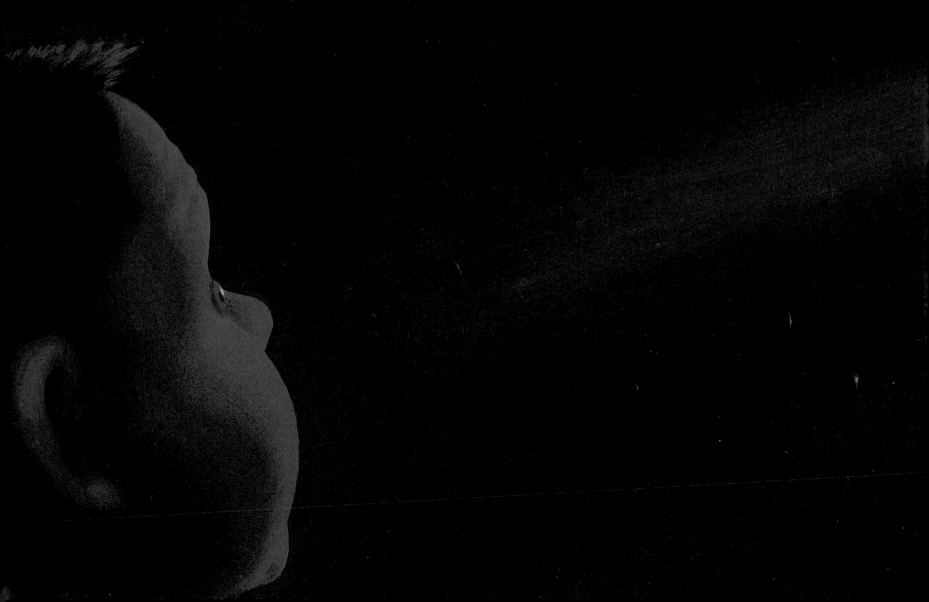

I can't describe this awful monster except to say that it looked exactly like—like the picture on the next page! Shall we turn the page—or is it too scary? Okay, if that's what you want.

"ARE YOU SCARED?"
the creature asked.

"**YES!**" I screamed
as I ran to the stairs.

"DON'T YOU HAVE
A QUESTION FOR ME?"
the creature said,
moving toward me.

"Yes," I said.
"What have you done with
Mr. Neewollah?"

"I ATE HIM!"
the creature laughed.
"HE IS INSIDE OF ME.
WOULD YOU LIKE TO
SEE HIM?"

"**No!**"
I yelled, and ran up the
stairs as fast as I could.

THE DOOR WAS LOCKED! I threw myself against it, but it didn't budge.

"STAY!" the creature commanded. "TURN AROUND AND SEE WHAT I HAVE DONE TO YOUR NEIGHBOR, MR. NEEWOLLAH!"

I turned and saw the monster grab his head and twist it. He struggled hard. He grunted. He groaned. It looked like he was trying to pull his head off. *Yiiiich!* I pounded on the door and yelled, **"HELP! HELP!"**

"STAY!!" he screamed
and started up the stairs.
I couldn't breathe . . .

Is it getting too scary for you? Should I keep
going? Okay, if you say so.

The monster came closer and closer. "GET ME OUT OF HERE!" he shouted.

"**NO!**" I shouted back, pounding the door. "**I'M GETTING *ME* OUT OF HERE!**"

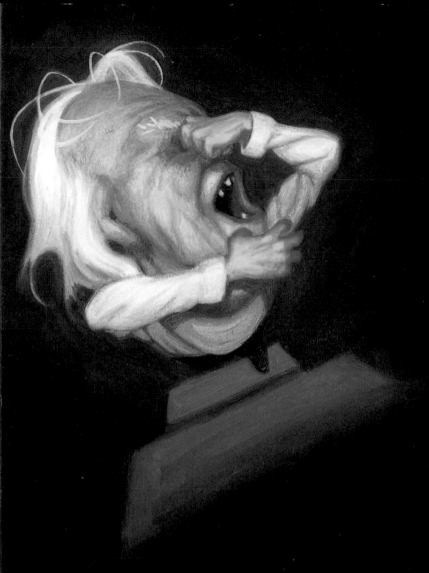

"NO!"
the monster yelled, tugging at his neck.
"YOU MUST HELP ME!"

"**WHAT**?" I asked. This
monster sounded strangely
familiar now.

"UNSTICK THIS
DARN ZIPPER!!"
he screamed.

So I grabbed the monster's head and gave a frantic pull on the zipper. And there, as the head split open, was Mr. Neewollah, safe and sound.
IT WAS JUST A COSTUME!

"I SCARED YOU, DIDN'T I?" he asked.

"I feel silly," I laughed, weak with relief.

"SCARING PEOPLE IS WHAT I DO FOR A LIVING," he said. "WOULD YOU LIKE TO SEE MY SECRET WORKSHOP?"

"Isn't this it?" I asked.

"NO," he said, "COME ON!"

"**BE CAREFUL,**" he warned,
smiling his crooked smile. As
I took my first step, he hit
my shoulder and shouted
"**HEY!**"

I screamed and went tumbling
down, down, down . . . I landed
hard on my bottom. Mr. Neewollah
came running at me.

"Don't come one step closer!"
I yelled, raising my fist.
"You pushed me!"

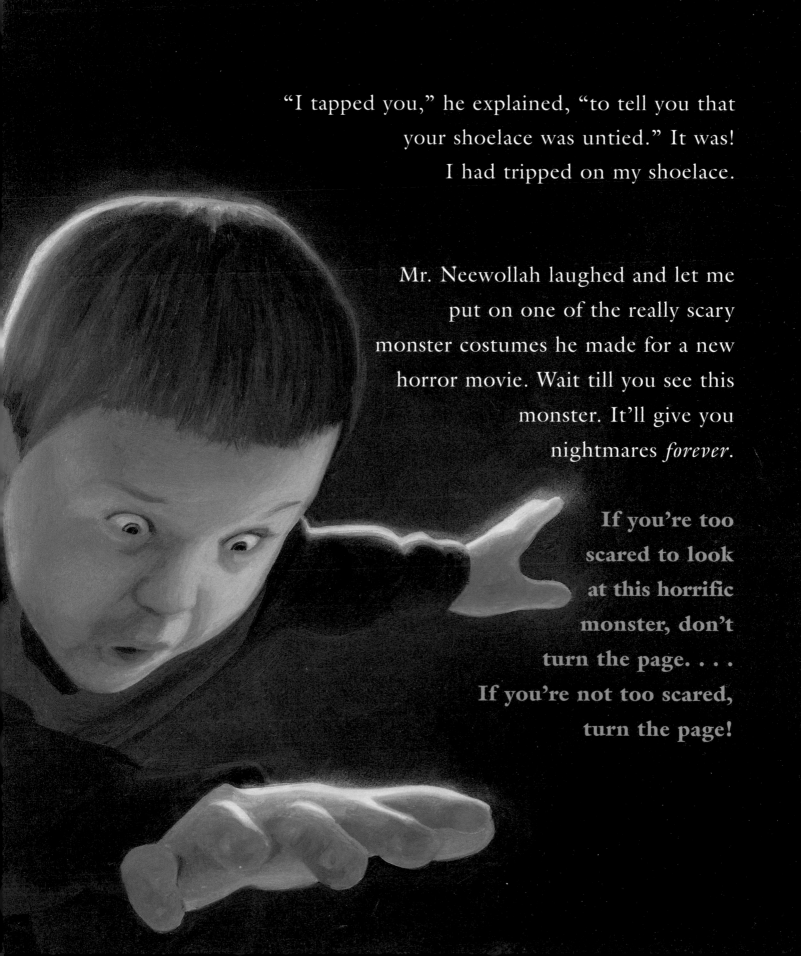

"I tapped you," he explained, "to tell you that your shoelace was untied." It was! I had tripped on my shoelace.

Mr. Neewollah laughed and let me put on one of the really scary monster costumes he made for a new horror movie. Wait till you see this monster. It'll give you nightmares *forever*.

If you're too scared to look at this horrific monster, don't turn the page. . . . If you're not too scared, turn the page!

"Boo!"

I scared Mr. Neewollah!

We both laughed. He let me keep the costume on and walked me

back home so I could frighten my mom and dad.

Boy, were they scared!

Say, were you wondering if "Neewollah" was Mr. Neewollah's
real name? I did, too. So I asked him.

Mr. Neewollah smiled and said, "I thought a smart person like you would have
figured out that Neewollah is **HALLOWEEN** spelled backward."
"Mr. Halloween!" I said, laughing. "I guess I'm not that smart."

But YOU are!